Effie

Beverley Allinson Barbara Reid

Scholastic Canada

Scholastic Canada Ltd.
175 Hillmount Road, Markham, Ontario L6C 1Z7

Scholastic Inc.
555 Broadway, New York, NY 10012, USA

Scholastic Australia Pty Limited
PO Box 579, Gosford, NSW 2250, Australia

Scholastic New Zealand Limited
Private Bag 94407, Greenmount,
Auckland, New Zealand

Scholastic Ltd.
Villiers House, Clarendon Avenue, Leamington Spa,
Warwickshire CV32 5PR, UK

Design: Many Pens Design Ltd.
Photography by Ian Crysler
First published by Summerhill Press Ltd., 1990

Cover photo of Barbara Reid by Ian Crysler
Cover photo of Beverley Allinson by Susan Gaitskell

Canadian Cataloguing in Publication Data

Allinson, Beverley, 1936-
     Effie

ISBN 0-590-74031-8

I. Reid, Barbara, 1957-. II. Title.

PS8551.L557E4 1992   jC813'.54   C91-095296-5
PZ7.A55Ef 1992

1 0 9 8 7 6 5   Printed in Hong Kong   2 3 4 5 6 / 0

Effie came from a long long line of ants.

She was an ant like hundreds of others—
in every way but one.

All the others had tiny ant voices.

Effie's voice was like thunder.

Whenever she spoke, the whole nest of ants
ran to get away from the noise.

One day, Effie set out to find someone who would listen to her. Before long a caterpillar wriggled into sight.

"NICE DAY, ISN'T IT?" said Effie.

But she was talking to thin air.
The caterpillar almost split his skin
in his hurry to escape.

Next minute, a butterfly landed beside her.

"HELLO THERE!" Effie boomed.

But the butterfly was blown away
and Effie was alone again. Disappointed, but still hopeful,
Effie climbed a grass stalk for a different view.

"WHERE IS SOMEONE TO TALK TO?" she wondered.

Her voice shook a web nearby
and a spider crawled out
to see what she had caught.

"HOW DO YOU DO? WHO ARE YOU?" Effie began.

Effie went on for a long time
without meeting anyone at all.
By and by she stopped to rest.

But the web snapped.
Without a word, the spider
parachuted to safety and was gone.

To her surprise,
the rock she was lying on
suddenly sprouted legs.
"HELLO THERE!" said Effie.
"HAVE YOU TIME FOR A CHAT?"

But the beetle flipped in fright.
He spun in a dizzy circle,
snapped to his feet
and scurried away.

When she met a grasshopper, all Effie said was, **"HI!"**

Even so, the grasshopper didn't stay.

"DOESN'T ANYONE WANT TO LISTEN TO ME?"

Effie yelled to the treetops.

Just then the grasshopper came leaping back.

"YOU'VE CHANGED YOUR MIND?"
said Effie hopefully.
But the grasshopper shook his head
and zigzagged out of sight.

Then the beetle ran her way.

"WELCOME BACK!"
said Effie with open arms.
But the beetle scurried silently past.

"HAVE YOU COME TO TALK TO ME?"
Effie asked the spider, who was next.
"At a time like this?"
gasped the spider, spinning by.

And the butterfly passed in a flap.

The caterpillar wiggled right up to Effie. "Run for your life!" *he puffed.*

Effie raced after them all.   She raced till she reached

the hundreds of ants who had run away from her that morning.

They were all crowded around their nest,
glancing fearfully into the sky.
Effie felt the ground shake.
She saw a spreading shadow cover the ground.
She looked up.

A huge foot was about to crush them all.

Effie took a deep breath.

"STOP!" she roared.
"HOLD IT RIGHT THERE."

"*Where?*" said an elephant,
looking around in surprise.

"HERE!" bellowed Effie.
"PLEASE WATCH WHERE YOU STEP."
"WATCH YOUR STEP!" echoed the other ants.

"*Oops,*" said the elephant, suddenly noticing them all below.
"Sorry," she said and stepped nimbly aside.
Effie whooped and the ants cheered faintly as the elephant's foot
and the near swish of her trunk missed them all.

"Who spoke up?" asked the elephant.

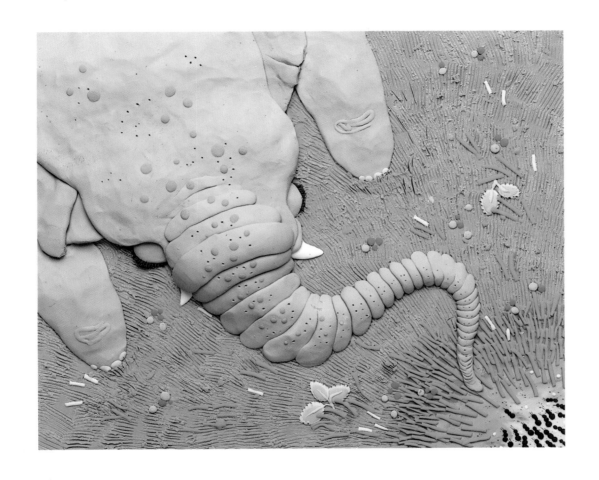

Effie waved an antenna to introduce herself
and the elephant lowered her trunk to the ground in greeting.

Effie climbed up, as if the trunk were a staircase,
until she and the elephant saw eye to eye.

"I DON'T SUPPOSE YOU HAVE TIME FOR A CHAT?" she asked.

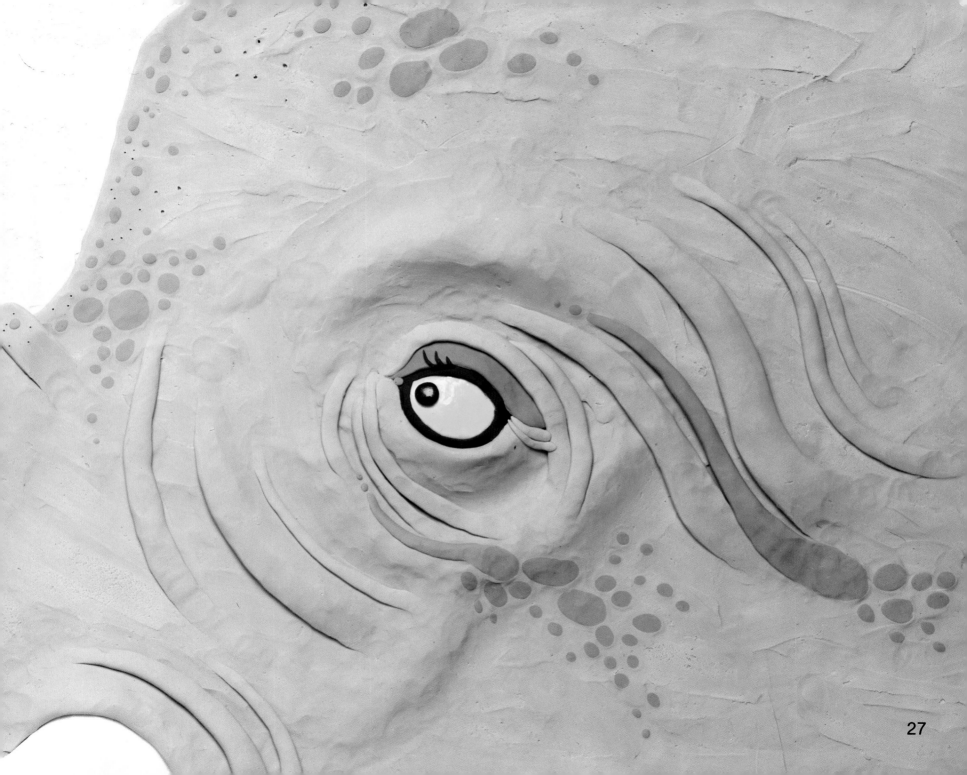

Effie and the elephant found they liked each other enormously.

They talked for the rest of the day.

And for days and weeks and months after,
they met to talk of things large and small.

Before too long, large numbers of elephants could be seen
treading carefully through the grass, watching their step
and chatting with their new friends.